# YO-KAI WATCH

## The Misadventures of Jibanyan

Adapted by Kate Howard

**SCHOLASTIC INC.**

©LEVEL-5/YWP. Produced by Scholastic Inc. under license from LEVEL-5.

Published by Scholastic Inc., *Publishers since 1920*. SCHOLASTIC and associated logos are trademarks and/or registered trademarks of Scholastic Inc.

ISBN 978-1-338-05462-0

10 9 8 7 6 5 4 3 2 1        16 17 18 19 20

Printed in the U.S.A.      40
First printing 2016

Nate was an ordinary fifth-grade kid—until he discovered the secret, invisible world of Yo-kai. Yo-kai are mischievous beings who *love* to create problems for the human world.

Got the wrong order at the drive-through? Can't find your homework that you *know* you put in your backpack? A Yo-kai is probably to blame.

Thanks to the Yo-kai Watch, Nate can see and communicate with these magical beings. With the guidance of his Yo-kai butler, Whisper, it's Nate's job to befriend the Yo-kai. He often calls upon his Yo-kai pals for help. But first, he has to win over each Yo-kai and get him or her to trust him.

This is the story of how Nate and a Yo-kai named Jibanyan became good friends—despite a few messy misadventures along the way!

# CHAPTER 1

"**Y**O-KAI REALLY *DO* EXIST?" Nate asked, flopping down on his bed. He still couldn't believe he had been given that magical watch in the woods. It seemed too strange to be true.

"Afraid so," Nate's Yo-kai guide, Whisper, replied. "The Yo-kai live in a dimension parallel to the human world. They often come to the human realm to cause trouble. The only thing is, no one can see them but you."

Nate sighed and gazed at his new watch. "I can't believe it."

"Don't worry, Nate." Whisper grinned. "As long as I'm here, you can rest easy. I will protect you from trouble, and maybe even make things better for you."

Nate gave him a look of disbelief. So far, Whisper hadn't proven to be much help at all.

Whisper zipped around Nate's head. "Oh, and P.S.: It's

impossible to take off the Yo-kai Watch. Your life is never going to be the same."

Nate shook his head. "What have I gotten myself into?" He stood up and headed outside. Whisper trailed along after him.

As they reached a busy intersection near Nate's house, Nate slowed down. He carefully looked both ways. Then he told Whisper, "Did you hear? Strange things are going on at this intersection."

"What kind of strange things?" Whisper asked.

"Near misses," Nate explained. "Way more than usual. Cars almost hitting people—"

"Hitting people?!" Whisper shrieked.

"But they stop just in time," Nate told him.

"Just in time?" Whisper gasped.

"That's why it's called a near miss," Nate said.

"Shouldn't that be called a near *hit*?" Whisper crossed his arms. He scanned the intersection. "This has got to be the work of a Yo-kai! A truly nefarious one must be inspiriting this intersection."

"Inspiriting?" Nate asked.

Whisper nodded. "It happens all the time. Inspiritings happen when a Yo-kai refuses to leave its place of demise." He glanced at his Yo-kai Pad. "Because it cannot accept the fact that it is no longer alive."

Nate peeked over Whisper's shoulder. "Are you reading off the Yo-kai wiki?! Isn't that kind of cheating?"

"It's just for reference," Whisper said huffily.

Nate lifted his eyebrows. "Sure it is."

"Moving on . . ." Whisper said. "Now, Nate, please go ahead and illuminate the Yo-kai hiding in the darkness with your Yo-kai Watch."

Nate flipped open his new watch. A beam of bright light shot out. Nate aimed it at the street in front of him. "I don't see anything."

"Keep searching. You can't see the Yo-kai unless it is hit directly by the light," Whisper said.

Nate shone the light first left, and then right. Suddenly, he and Whisper both gasped.

"There it is!" Whisper pointed. "That must be the vile monster."

A dark shadow rose up into the air and roared at them. Nate and Whisper took a step backward. The Yo-kai inspiriting the intersection was *terrifying*!

But when the light cleared, Nate blinked. "Huh?"

An adorable orange-and-white kitty meowed at them. "Jibanyan!" he purred. The little cat yawned, scratched his bottom, and began licking his paws.

"*That's* the vile monster?" Nate said.

Whisper consulted the Yo-kai wiki. "It says here that his name is Jibanyan."

"Meow," Jibanyan said sweetly.

A well-dressed businessman walked toward the intersection. Then he stopped to wait for a break in traffic before he crossed.

Suddenly, Jibanyan leaped to his feet and jumped *into* the man. The kitten took over the guy's body, leading him straight into the street.

*"Meow!"* Jibanyan hissed from inside the man's body. "Meow, meow!"

"What's happening?" Nate asked in alarm.

"The man is inspirited!" Whisper said.

A truck was speeding toward the intersection. It was headed straight for the man!

Nate waved his arms wildly. "Look out!"

Whisper covered his eyes. He couldn't watch.

But just before the truck struck the man, Jibanyan jumped out

of his body and flew at the truck with his fists flying.

"Meow!" the Yo-kai screeched. "Take that, stupid truck! Paws of Fury! *Nya nya nya!*"

Jibanyan pounded at the truck. Before it hit the man, it crashed into Jibanyan, and then screeched to a stop. The little Yo-kai was launched up into the air—and the man was left unharmed.

The truck driver leaned out the window. "What are you doing?!" he shouted at the man.

"My legs moved on their own," the man said.

"That was a close call," Nate murmured.

Whisper nodded. "So that explains all these near

misses you were talking about. Looks like Jibanyan has been possessing people and walking into traffic."

"Can we stop him?" Nate asked.

Whisper shrugged. "Negotiation or confrontation?"

Just then, Jibanyan crashed to the ground at Nate's feet. "Meow," the cat said softly.

"Meow to you," Whisper replied.

"Meow?" Jibanyan asked.

"Meow to you," Whisper said again.

Jibanyan spun around, his eyes bulging out of his furry little head. "Can you guys really see me?"

"Uh, sort of . . ." Nate said.

"How is that possible?" Jibanyan screeched. "Do you know little Amy?"

Nate shook his head. "Who?"

*"Nyo nyo nyo!"* Jibanyan screamed. "I'm *nyot* ready yet!"

"Help is available," Whisper said, pointing at Nate. "From this guy! Nate!"

"Dude?" Nate said, obviously annoyed. "What the—?"

"We have to stop these near misses," Whisper reminded him. "Right?"

"Oh yeah," Nate said. "Right. So tell me, Jibanyan. Why are you doing this anyway?"

"Meow," Jibanyan said sadly. "When I was alive, my owner, Amy, took care of me and loved me. We used to sleep in bed, on the couch, under the table . . . Oh, I was so happy back then."

"But all you did was sleep," Nate pointed out.

"Well, he *is* a cat," Whisper said.

Jibanyan sighed. "One day, I was hit by a truck. There was no pain. Suddenly, I was a Yo-kai." With tears in his eyes, the Yo-kai continued, "I heard Amy say, 'I can't believe you let yourself get hit by a truck . . . *so lame*!'"

Nate and Whisper exchanged a look.

"What a heartless monster!" Whisper said.

"*Nyo!*" Jibanyan blubbered. "*Nyo*, she isn't! Amy loves me. And she wouldn't have said I was lame if I hadn't gotten hit by a car!" He took a deep breath. "That's why I'm training myself to become a cat who can defeat any car."

"But you can't go around inspiriting people," Nate told him. "It's dangerous."

"Hmm," Jibanyan purred. "I never thought about that." He looked out into the street. His eyes lit up when he saw a truck flying toward the intersection. "I'll just do it all by myself!"

Jibanyan dashed into the intersection . . . and was hit by the truck! It threw him high into the sky.

When Jibanyan landed, he dusted himself off. "Okay, that didn't go as planned. I think I *nyeed* to stretch first."

Whisper smirked. "Yes, it's important to stretch before getting hit by a car."

"Okay," Jibanyan said. "I think I got it this time!" He jumped in front of another truck. Once again, he was thrown into the air.

"Man," Nate said, cringing. "There are a lot of trucks here today."

Jibanyan flung himself at truck after truck. "Paws of Fury!" he screamed. *"Nya nya nya nya!"*

But no matter how fierce he made himself look—or how fast his Paws of Fury flew—every truck that passed sent Jibanyan flying.

Jibanyan splatted onto the sidewalk again and again. "See? It doesn't work if I do it by myself."

"Gee," Whisper said, "I wonder why you can't stop trucks all by yourself."

"Because I'm too lonely," Jibanyan said. He wandered out into the street. "I'm so lonely all the time, and when I'm with someone else, I don't feel afraid. That's why I inspirit people." Tears streamed down his face. "I'm sorry I'm such a troublemaker. I guess I'll just be alone forever!" he sobbed.

"Wait—Jibanyan?" Nate called after him.

Jibanyan stopped and spun around. "Meow?"

"If you want to ..." Nate gulped. "You can inspirit me. I'd be happy to train with you."

"Why would you do that?" Jibanyan asked, his eyes hopeful.

Nate shrugged. "Because I think it's amazing you're working so hard to win Amy back. Jibanyan, I can tell you must love her very, very much."

"Meow," Jibanyan squeaked through his tears.

"Let's hang out together," Nate said. "You know, we can be friends."

"Meow!" Jibanyan smiled happily. His fur began to glow, and then a little silver medal appeared over the kitten's head. It landed in Nate's open palm.

"What is this?" Nate asked, studying the medal.

"A Yo-kai Medal," Whisper told him. "It's a symbol of your friendship with a Yo-kai!"

Nate wrapped his fingers around the medal. Suddenly, he, too, began to glow.

Jibanyan beamed at him. "We're friends now. Friends forever!"

"Awesome!" Nate said. He held out his arms, and Jibanyan ran toward him. "Jibanyan!"

"*Nyate!*" Jibanyan meowed back.

"Jibanyan!" Nate said.

"*Nyate!*" Jibanyan meowed again.

But before the little cat could reach his new friend, another truck came screeching through the intersection. It smashed into Jibanyan, and he flew up into the sky.

Nate shook his head. "He's hopeless."

# CHAPTER 2

## HERE COMES ROUGHRAFF

A FEW DAYS LATER, Nate got his first chance to try out Jibanyan's Yo-kai Medal. A new Yo-kai had turned up at school, and he was creating all kinds of trouble for Nate's friend Eddie.

Eddie was one of the best students in the fifth grade. But suddenly he'd started acting *very* naughty. Kicking walls, acting like he hated school, picking on his classmates . . . it was extremely un-Eddie-like behavior!

"There's got to be a Yo-kai involved here," Nate said.

"Unless Eddie has gone insane," Whisper suggested.

Nate snuck up behind Eddie. He shined his Yo-kai Watch into the shadows around his classmate. The light soon illuminated a figure lurking behind Eddie.

"Gotcha, dude," Nate said, beaming.

"Not this guy . . ." Whisper moaned when he saw who it was. "It's Roughraff. He's a Yo-kai who makes good kids go bad."

As Nate and Whisper watched, Roughraff licked his lips and smirked.

"Roughraff is public enemy number one. He's responsible for ninety-eight percent of the troublemakers worldwide," Whisper explained.

"We've got to stop him!" Nate narrowed his eyes. "Roughraff, I'm coming for you!"

Roughraff laughed. "Ooh, I'm shaking in my boots! Catch me if you can." He jumped onto an imaginary motorcycle, revved his fake engine, and zoomed away.

"He left Eddie," Nate moaned, watching Roughraff zip off. "And Eddie isn't back to normal!"

Whisper consulted the Yo-kai wiki on his Y-Pad. "Roughraff's influence is a hard habit to break. Eddie won't change back until we defeat him!"

Nate and Whisper hurried after the bad-boy Yo-kai.

"Ready to go rotten?" Roughraff taunted when they found him in a park near Nate's house.

Ready to go rotten?

"We'll see, Roughraff," Nate said. He slid Jibanyan's medal into the watch. "Come out, my friend. Calling Jibanyan! Yo-kai Medal, do your thing!"

Jibanyan was summoned from the watch.

"Jibanyan, go teach Roughraff a lesson!" Nate ordered him.

Jibanyan studied his fellow Yo-kai. "Meow?"

"Gotta get rough!" Roughraff growled. He launched himself at Jibanyan. Then he flipped himself onto the cat's shoulders.

Suddenly, both Yo-kai began to glow. A second later, smoke surrounded them.

"No!" Nate shouted when he realized what was happening. Roughraff was using his powers on Jibanyan!

When the smoke cleared, Roughraff was gone . . . and Jibanyan had changed.

"It's good to be bad!" he drawled, spinning around.

"He's gone to the dark side!" Nate said.

"Jibanyan?" Whisper asked.

"*Nyo* one here with that name anymore," the cat formerly known as Jibanyan purred. "My name is . . . Baddinyan. I don't care about my bad reputation." Baddinyan chuckled. "And if you don't believe me . . . just watch. Heh."

"Don't do something you'll regret," Whisper warned.

Baddinyan pulled two chocobars out of his pocket and started eating them both . . . at the same time. "That's right. Two chocobars!" he sneered.

Whisper gasped. "Right before dinner?"

"That's how I roll." Baddinyan laughed. Suddenly, a bed appeared next to him. "*Nyow* I'm eating candy in bed."

Whisper threw his arms in the air. "What about the crumbs?!"

"*Nyo* trash cans? *Nyo* problem!" Baddinyan threw his candy wrappers onto the ground.

"Who's going to pick that up?" Whisper asked.

"And *nyow* I'm playing on the bed," Baddinyan said.

Who's going to pick that up?

He rolled back and forth over the neatly made bed, tangling up the covers.

Whisper put his face in his hands. "Your mother just made that bed!"

Baddinyan glanced at his paws. "Chocolate on my paws? Too bad I *won't be washing them*! Or brushing my teeth!"

"I can't watch anymore," Whisper whimpered.

"Ha!" Baddinyan snickered. "I'm bad to the bone. Do you feel me *nyow*?"

"Dude, you're embarrassing yourself!" Nate shook his head. He'd earned the Jibanyan medal by befriending him. But now that Baddinyan was in the picture, Nate's new Yo-kai pal was causing a whole lot more trouble than Nate had bargained for.

Nate sighed. He couldn't help wondering what would happen the next time Jibanyan turned up.

# CHAPTER 3

## LET'S EXORCISE

**T**HOUGH **J**IBANYAN EVENTUALLY returned to his usual, cuddly self, Nate's troubles with the mischievous Yo-kai were far from over.

"Nate!" Nate's mom called from the kitchen. "Who ate our artisanal Swiss chocolate bars?"

"I don't know," Nate said. "It wasn't me."

Nate's mom looked at him suspiciously. "I told you, Nate. You're not supposed to snack before dinner."

"Really, Mom," Nate promised. "It wasn't me!"

"Honestly?" his mom said, looking up from the stove. "Gosh, I'm sorry, Nate. I could have sworn we had some left. I bet it was your dad …"

Nate slipped out of the kitchen. As he made his way upstairs, he murmured to Whisper, "I think there's a Yo-kai around here who's been eating all my mom's chocobars."

"But that's not possible," Whisper said. "I have a nose for Yo-kai, and I smell nothing."

Nate paused before opening the door to his room. Whisper chuckled. "Don't you think that I would know about it if there was a Yo-kai in this house?"

Nate pushed open his bedroom door—and found Jibanyan lounging on his bed. The little cat yawned and rolled onto his back.

Nate gave Whisper a pointed look. "What's *that*, then?"

Jibanyan munched on a chocobar and snuggled deeper into Nate's covers.

"Are you kidding me?" Nate said. "Eating chocobars? Jibanyan, what are you doing here?"

Jibanyan looked up from the book he'd been

reading. "I've got some good *nyews*, *Nyate*. I've decided to *live* here!"

Good news, *Nyate*!

"What!" Nate and Whisper spat out at the same time.

"In *my* bedroom?" Nate asked.

"Listen, Jibanyan," Whisper cried. "You're making a big mistake. I know this seems like party central, but Nate is a terrible roommate. He snores, he's stinky, and he never cleans up after himself. And he never wants to stay up late, just talking!"

Jibanyan purred. "Eh, seems good to me."

Whisper was horrified. "Well, you can't live here and I'll tell you why. It's because there's already a prominent

Yo-kai living here. A Yo-kai butler named Whisper and he's not ready to share!"

Jibanyan flicked his tail at Whisper. "I don't see any problem. Meow."

"Were you even listening to me?" Whisper whimpered.

Jibanyan licked his paw. "Honestly? *Nyot* really."

"I'm asking you nicely!" Whisper begged. "Jibanyan?"

Jibanyan rolled around on Nate's bed, singing. *"I am a cat, and I like it like that. I wash my butt in a Laundromat!"*

"I refuse to be replaced by an ANNOYING CAT!" Whisper screamed. Then he launched himself at Jibanyan, who lazily rolled away.

"Hey, hold on a second, Whisper," Nate said, tugging his Yo-kai friend away from Jibanyan. "Aren't you acting a little undignified for a butler?"

Whisper backed away from the cat. "I apologize for my uncouth behavior," he wheezed.

Nate studied him. "Not buying it. Look, dude, I'll just handle this. Jibanyan, why do you want to live here anyway?"

"He won't answer you," Whisper said, crossing his arms. "The cat's rude."

Jibanyan smiled up at Nate. With big, innocent eyes, he said, "I'll tell *you* why, Nyate . . ."

"Oh, now you're just making *me* look bad!" Whisper huffed, punching at a pillow. "Leave. Leave. Leave!"

Leave! Leave! Leave!

Jibanyan sulked. "I got kicked out of my home!"

"Really?" Nate asked, curious. He thought he was the only one who could exert any power over the Yo-kai! "How?"

"I was living *nyear* the intersection," Jibanyan explained. "But one day when I got home . . . a big mean cat had stolen my spot!" He hung his head. "Apparently, there has been a sharp increase in cat-type Yo-kai, which has caused a serious housing shortage." Jibanyan shrugged. "And they didn't want to share the rent. So I came here to live with you."

"That doesn't make sense," Whisper insisted. "In fact, it's complete nonsense. There is only room for one Yo-kai in this house, and that Yo-kai is *me!*"

"Hold on, Whisper," Nate said. "Don't you feel bad for Jibanyan at all? He's homeless."

"Are you *kidding* me?" Whisper sighed.

Are you *kidding* me?

Nate gave him a firm look. Then he turned to Jibanyan. "My mom and dad can't see Yo-kai, so as long as you don't bother anyone and you follow the rules, you can live here for as long as you want to. Does that sound good to you?"

"Oh, *Nyate*," Jibanyan purred. "Really?"

"Of course, Jibanyan." Nate smiled. "You're my friend."
"I'll be good! I promise!" Jibanyan cheered.

But no matter how hard Jibanyan *tried* to stay out of
trouble, he just couldn't seem to help it.

First, he stole Nate's mom's chocobars. He even tried
to sneak them out of the kitchen right under her nose!

"Huh?" Nate's mom said, spinning around. "What . . .?"

Nate grabbed the chocolate bars from Jibanyan's
paws. His mom rubbed her eyes.

"Something wrong, Mom?" Nate asked as Jibanyan
scooted out of the kitchen.

His mom went back to her paperwork. "I think all
these bills are making me see things."

Nate laughed nervously. Then he raced out of the kitchen. "Jibanyan, you promised! You said you'd be good."

Jibanyan grinned. "Wasn't me."

"Do you want to get evicted?" Nate snapped.

Jibanyan stuck chocobars into his ears. "I can't *hear* you, *Nyate!*" he sang. *"I am a cat, and I like it like that!"*

Nate shook his fist in frustration.

Later that afternoon, Nate's mom stood outside the bathroom door. "Nate, are you in there?" she asked.

Someone knocked back at her from inside the bathroom.

"I'm right here," Nate said, coming up behind his mom.

His mom looked from Nate to the door and back again. "If you're out here, then who's in *there?*"

Through the door, Nate could hear Jibanyan singing, *"I'm a cat, and I like it like that . . ."*

"Uh, no one," said Nate. "Um, Mom, come with me. There's something I have to show you in the other room . . ."

That night, Nate's dad began having trouble with the TV. "This is crazy!" he said, pounding at the remote control.

"What's wrong, Dad?" Nate asked.

"No matter what I press, all I get is this girl band, Next HarMEOWny!" Nate's dad said angrily.

Nate glanced at the TV. Jibanyan was punching at the buttons along the side.

"Paws of Fury!" he cried. "Show me the girls!"

Nate glared at him, and Jibanyan smiled sweetly back.

No matter how many times Nate pleaded with him, Jibanyan just kept acting naughty.

Back in his bedroom, Nate stood over Jibanyan. "I don't know what you think you're doing, Jibanyan, but these pranks have got to stop. Do you understand me?"

"They're *nyot* pranks, *Nyate*," Jibanyan explained. "That's just how I roll."

Whisper floated over Jibanyan. "You do know that Nate will kick you out if you don't behave?"

"I get it now. I'm sorry. I'll behave. I promise." Jibanyan smirked. "Starting tomorrow." He pulled out a chocobar and munched noisily.

Nate shook his head. "This is not going to end well."

A minute later, Nate's parents stepped into the room.

"Nate?" his dad said. "Do you have a minute? We've hired a paranormal investigator to help us figure out what's been going on around here."

"What?" Nate said, his eyes growing wide.

A strange man appeared in the doorway.

"Please do this room first," Nate's mom said, waving the investigator in.

"This guy's a total quack," Whisper said quietly to Nate. "Where'd they find him, on the Internet? There's no way he can see Yo-kai."

The small man held up a long staff and waved it around. Then he began to chant:

*"Starlight, star bright,*
*Rid this house of ghosts tonight.*
*Eye of newt and horn of toad,*
*Let this home be free of spirit load.*
*By the power of three times three, I will smite thee.*
*Bibbidi-bobbidi-bee."*

Nate rolled his eyes. But then Jibanyan began to float up toward a beam of light shining from the ceiling!

"Wait ..." Nate said, staring at Jibanyan. "It's *working*?!"

The investigator continued to chant:

*"Zippity zappity, flippity flappity.*

*Rid this house of all that's unhappity."*

Whisper began to float up, too. "It's so beautiful," he said, soaring toward the glowing light.

"Whisper, too?" Nate murmured. He reached for both Yo-kai. "Don't go into the light!"

It's so beautiful ...

"A boom-chakalaka, boom-chakalaka, ghosts be gone!" the man chanted.

"My gosh," Whisper said as the light grew brighter. "It's full of stars."

"Oh no!" Nate said desperately. "I've got to do something!"

He stuck a platter of pastries in front of the investigator. "Excuse me, sir—would you like some scones?"

The man put down his staff and stopped chanting. "Huh? Thank you! How thoughtful!"

Would you like some scones?

Jibanyan and Whisper both sighed and floated down toward the floor again.

"Nate," Nate's mom said. "Let the man work."

"Oh," Nate said. "Sorry . . ."

The man began to chant once more:

*"Ring around the rosy,*

*Pocketful of nosey . . . ghosts!"*

Nate watched helplessly as Whisper and Jibanyan floated up, up, up. "Not again!" he cried. He stepped toward the man. "Oh, hey. You need a massage, sir!"

The light overhead faded again, and the Yo-kai drifted back down toward the ground.

"I feel much better now," the investigator said, smiling at Nate. Then he resumed his chant. *"Evil spirits, leave this place!"*

Though Whisper and Jibanyan tried to fight it, the pull of the light was just too strong. They both floated upward toward the light as the man chanted:

*"In-a-gadda-da-vida! Bobbidi-bee!"*

Nate knew he had to do something. Whisper and Jibanyan were about to disappear into the great beyond. He'd never see them again! He was desperate.

Nate looked at the man. "Whoa! You did it!" He began spinning around the room. "The energy in here feels so clean! Those ghosts are definitely gone. I feel completely refreshed! My aura, it's glowing. Whatever you did, it worked. It really did."

The investigator lowered his staff and looked around the room. "Yes, you're right. They are all gone now."

Nate sighed happily. "Whatever they're paying you, totally worth it," he said.

As soon as Nate's parents and the investigator were gone, Jibanyan and Whisper crashed to the floor of Nate's bedroom.

"That was a close one, Nate," Whisper said. "He almost got us!"

Nate smiled at his two friends. He realized how sad he would have been if the Yo-kai were gone. Jibanyan could be a menace, and Whisper a nuisance, but Nate was getting used to having them around!

The next day, Jibanyan was eager to prove he could be a good houseguest.

"Oh, Nate!" Nate's mom said when he went down for breakfast. "Who washed these dishes?"

Nate shrugged.

Then his dad came into the room. "Did you polish my golf clubs, Nate?"

Nate spun around. He spotted Jibanyan smiling at him from across the room. "Uh, yeah ..." Nate said. "Sort of."

Jibanyan scrubbed at the floor with a rag. *"Meow, meow, meow. I'm a good boy, I'm a good boy,"* he sang.

Whisper and Nate exchanged a look. "So tell me," Whisper said, "how long do you think this will last?"

Jibanyan meowed happily.

Nate shrugged. "I'm not holding my breath ..."

# CHAPTER 4

 ## YO-KAI HIDABAT

A FEW DAYS LATER, Nate pounded on his locked bedroom door. "Are you in there, Jibanyan? I'm late for soccer!"

"Leave me alone, *Nyate*," Jibanyan said sadly from the other side of the door. The little Yo-kai was curled up on Nate's bed, sulking. "I just want to be left alone. Alone in the dark."

"But this is my room!" Nate said, groaning. He knocked again. "Hello?"

Whisper craned his neck. "Wait a second! Can you hear that?"

"Hear what?" Nate asked.

"Of course!" Whisper jabbed his finger into the air. "It must be ultrasonic. Far too high-pitched for humans to hear."

"What are you talking about?" Nate asked.

Whisper stuck out his lips and made an annoying sound. "*BZZZ BZZZ.*"

"Hmm," Nate said. "I can't hear anything."

Whisper pulled out his Yo-kai Pad. "Yup, here it is," he said, pointing at the screen. "These ultrasonic waves are almost certainly being emitted by the Yo-kai Hidabat."

"Hidabat?" Nate asked.

"Yes," Whisper said, scratching his

head. "It's the Yo-kai who makes the inspirited lock themselves away from the rest of the world, afraid to come out at all. They sit there in the dark, alone. You probably don't know this, but Hidabat's influence has been growing steadily these last few years."

"*I* probably didn't know it?" Nate said. "*You* were just reading it."

You were just reading it.

Whisper laughed nervously and hid the tablet behind his back.

"So you're telling me that Jibanyan has been inspirited by this Hidabat character and that's why he won't come out?" Nate said.

Whisper nodded. "That is correct."

Nate groaned. He was already late to meet his friends. "But my soccer ball is in my room! Jibanyan, come out!"

"That's Hidabat for you," Whisper said wisely. "He's a creature that lurks in the shadows and is not so easy to reason with."

Nate brightened. "Wait, I know how to get Jibanyan out of my room!" He pulled out two chocobars. "Jibanyan? How about some delicious chocobars? I've got your favorite ..."

"Available for a limited time only!" Whisper chimed in.

"Just leave them there, *Nyate*," Jibanyan called sadly from inside the room. "I'll eat them later."

"He won't even come out for chocobars?" Nate said, shocked. Then he had another idea. He reached into his backpack and pulled out a magazine. "Jibanyan! Ooh, wow. Look what came in the mail for you! The new issue of your fanzine is here with exclusive backstage photos of Next HarMEOWny. Oh no, there's tension brewing behind the scenes!"

"The girls are fighting and they might break up!" Whisper cried.

That was enough to get Jibanyan to open the door

Look what came in the mail!

just a crack. He peeked out, grabbed the chocobars and magazine, and then slammed the door shut again.

"Great," Whisper moaned. "He definitely won't come out now that he's got his precious chocobars."

"You're kidding me!" Nate said, thinking. "Now, *who* could persuade Jibanyan?" He pulled a Yo-kai Medal out of his collection and flipped it in the air.

"Are you *sure* you really want to call that guy?" Whisper asked.

"It's worth a shot," Nate said, shrugging. He held the medal up high. "Come on out, my friend! Calling . . . *BLAZION!* Yo-kai Medal, do your thing!"

The brave lion Yo-kai appeared before them. *"Blazion!"*

"Blazion," Nate said. "Can you help me get Jibanyan to come out of my room?"

"*RAR-RAR!*" Blazion roared at Nate's bedroom door.

"I'll never leave this room, *Nyate*." Jibanyan sighed. "What's the point? Nothing really matters."

Blazion continued pounding at the door.

"You can do it, Blazion!" Nate cheered.

"Don't give up!" Whisper urged.

Blazion roared and growled at the door. But it was no use. No matter how much he roared, Jibanyan wasn't coming out.

Blazion yelped in frustration. Then he ran downstairs, out the door, and all the way down the street.

"I need someone else," Nate said desperately. "I know! We need Yo-kai *DISMARELDA* and *HAPPIERRE*!"

Nate summoned the happy Yo-kai couple.

"I'm so not in the mood for this," Dismarelda grumbled when Nate told them why he needed their help.

"Such a pleasure to see you, Nate!" Happierre said.

"This seems hopeless," Dismarelda groaned. "Are we even up for this, babe?"

"If we work together," Happierre said hopefully, "I think so! Come on, it'll be fun!"

The two enormous Yo-kai slithered under Nate's door.

"*Bonjour*, sunshine," Happierre told Jibanyan.

"We're here to cheer you up," Dismarelda told the glum kitty cat.

A few moments later, the pair of Yo-kai slid Jibanyan out from under the door of Nate's room.

"Jibanyan!" Nate said happily.

Dismarelda and Happierre bounced away, happy to have helped.

As soon as they were gone, Jibanyan hung his shoulders. He banged his head into the door of Nate's room. He was desperate to get back to his hiding place.

"Jibanyan must still be inspirited by Hidabat!" Whisper told Nate.

"All right," Nate said, pulling out another Yo-kai Medal. "Here goes nothing! Calling . . . *FIDGEPHANT*! Yo-kai Medal, do your thing!"

Fidgephant appeared before them. This Yo-kai was very good at getting people and Yo-kai to let go.

"So much pressure . . . let it out!" the little elephant Yo-kai sang. He held up his trunk and sprayed Jibanyan with his magic.

Hidabat appeared, and the two inspirited Yo-kai rushed to the bathroom. Nate's plan had worked!

"He came out!" Nate whooped.

But as soon as they came back, Hidabat wrapped his wings around Jibanyan again.

"No! It's too scary, must hide!" Hidabat screamed.

"What are you doing?" Nate yelled, pulling him away from Jibanyan. "Leave him alone, Hidabat!"

"But I can't help it," Hidabat whined. "It's my nature to seek seclusion."

"Then please go hide yourself away, but leave my friend alone," Nate pleaded.

Hidabat sulked. "That's easy for you to say. The world is so scary these days. There's no place to hide anymore."

"It's hard for some Yo-kai to live in this world, Nate," Whisper explained.

"That's true, *Nyate*," Jibanyan said, nodding.

"I see your point," Nate said. "Hey! Maybe you could hide in the closet in my room. I mean, if you want to ..."

The three Yo-kai looked at Nate, surprised.

"Are you sure?" Hidabat asked.

"It's not a problem," Nate told him. "As long as you let us leave."

"We'll be roommates from *nyow* on!" Jibanyan said happily.

Hidabat smiled. "Oh, thank you! And here, please take this as rent. We're friends now."

"Your Yo-kai Medal?" Nate asked. "Totally cool. Now you're in my supernatural entourage!"

Nate held up the medal proudly, and then reached for the doorknob to his room. "Um, wait a second . . . the door's still locked. What about my soccer ball?"

"Just leave it to me, Nate," Whisper said. He passed straight through the door to Nate's room.

Nate gaped at the door for a minute.

"Wait, you can just pass right through doors?!" he shouted.

"Of course," Whisper called from inside. "Isn't it obvious?"

A second later, the door swung open, and Whisper waved Nate inside. "Welcome to your humble abode."

Nate whacked Whisper with a fan. "Why didn't you just do that in the first place?"

Whisper shrugged. "You never asked!"

# CHAPTER 5

 ## ROBONYAN ACTIVATE

"THIS MOVIE IS SO AWESOME!" Nate whooped. He, Whisper, and Jibanyan were watching a movie about robots on TV.

"What is a robot, *Nyate*?" Jibanyan asked.

"It's a mechanized humanoid from the future with advanced combat abilities and weaponry," Nate replied.

"Oh, I've got news for you, Nate," Whisper told him. "Yo-kai can be mechanized as well."

Jibanyan covered his eyes. "I don't ever want to be turned into a robot, meow."

"Why not?" Nate asked.

"Because if I were a machine, *nyo* one would want to be my friend," Jibanyan explained.

Late that night, long after Whisper and Nate had gone up to bed, Jibanyan was snoozing on the couch. Suddenly, he was jarred awake by the sound of stomping metal.

Jibanyan yawned and rolled over, muttering, "Are you still watching TV? Turn it down, *Nyate*."

But when Jibanyan opened his eyes, he saw it wasn't the TV making noise— it was a robot! "Meow? Is this a dream?"

"Negative," the robot droned. "This is no dream."

Jibanyan leaped up. "Meow meow meow meow meow!" He ran up the stairs and pounced onto Nate's bed. "Wake up, *Nyate*! There's a monster in the house!"

Nate rubbed his eyes. "What is it, Jibanyan?"

"Hurry!" Jibanyan dragged Nate downstairs. He pointed into the darkness. There were big robo-footprints on the floor.

"Footprints!" Whisper gasped.

Nate's eyes bulged. "What the—? It made holes in the floor!"

"We have to find it, *Nyate*!" Jibanyan exclaimed.

"Yeah," Nate agreed. "Or my mom is gonna kill me."

Nate and his Yo-kai pals followed the footprints outside. "This way!" Nate cried.

The trail led them all the way to the end of the block. There, the three friends came face-to-face with the metal creature.

"Who are you?" Nate asked.

"*Watashi wa* Robonyan," the robot replied in a loud, machinelike voice.

"What's with the weird voice?" Nate asked.

The robot tried a different voice. "Is this voice more pleasing to you?" he said in a country accent. Then he spoke in French. *"Parlez-vous français?"* And then he used an Australian accent. "G'day mate." And finally, he spoke in a voice that was robotic, but somehow conversational. "Greetings. Is this better?"

"A lot," Nate said, nodding. "How did you do that thing with all the different voices anyway?"

"I have been programmed to replicate many different vocal patterns to communicate with a wide variety of humans," the robot replied.

It looks just like me!

Jibanyan stared at the robot, horrified. "Don't you guys notice anything unusual about this robot? It looks just like me!"

Nate gaped at his Yo-kai pal, and then turned to look at the robot. "That's crazy!"

"They are quite similar if you look closely," Whisper noted.

"You *just* noticed that?!" Jibanyan pouted.

"Allow me to explain. I am Robonyan, a robot from the future," the robot said seriously. "I am you, Jibanyan."

Jibanyan backed up. "Ahhh . . . what do you mean, you're me?"

"Jibanyan, as a Yo-kai, you will live for many, many years. Humans do not live as long. In the future, the mysterious disappearance of a Yo-kai friend . . ." Robonyan looked pointedly at Whisper.

". . . leads to your choice to evolve. By fusing your Yo-kai spirit with advanced technology, you will become a Yo-kai robot. Robonyan. Me."

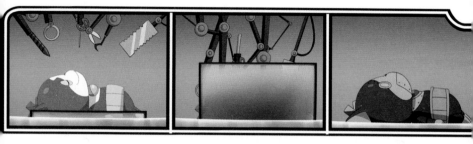

Jibanyan gasped. "You really *are* me? I can't believe it!"

"Then observe the evidence." Robonyan opened his mouth, and dozens of chocobars flowed out. "I—meaning, *you*—had a chocolate factory installed in this robot body. You are the only one who would have built me this way."

Jibanyan stuffed his face with chocobars. "Delicious, mmmm! You really *are* me!" He stopped chewing. "But I don't want to be a robot. I like the way I am *nyow* more than I like chocobars." He walked over and tapped on Robonyan's forehead. "Your body isn't soft. You can't walk stealthily. There's *nyothing* catlike about you!"

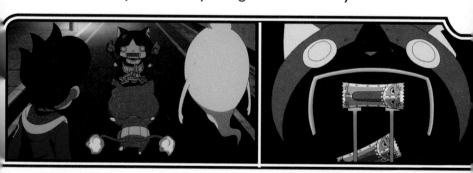

Robonyan glared at Jibanyan. "You can judge my value by competing against me. We will engage in a friendly race."

"You're toast!" Jibanyan said, certain he could race faster than his robot self.

You're toast!

"Okay, are you ready? And . . . GO!" Nate called out.

Jibanyan sped off the starting line. Robonyan stood there for a moment. Then the robot whispered, "Transform."

Suddenly, the little robot cat turned into a giant race car! It raced down the road and flew past Jibanyan, crossing the finish line first.

"Whoa!" Nate said. "Robonyan can totally transform!"

Robonyan shrugged. "It's a basic program every robot has."

"Look at me," Jibanyan shouted, making a goofy face. "I can transform, too, *Nyate!*"

Nate shook his head. "Dude, now you're just embarrassing yourself."

Jibanyan stomped his paw. "You may know how to transform, Robonyan, but I've got the eye of the tiger. Let's see how you do in the Yo-kai challenge!"

He led Robonyan to his favorite intersection. A truck

raced toward them. Jibanyan focused. "I've been training for this for a long time. Paws of Fury!"

But before Jibanyan could do his thing, Robonyan put out a single finger and stopped the truck.

Moments later, a second truck slammed into Jibanyan. The little cat flew into the sky.

When he landed, Jibanyan shook himself off. "All right, robo-me, you've been asking for this!" he growled. He raced toward Robonyan, swinging his fists as he cried, "Paws of Fury! *Nya nya nya nya nya nya!*"

But the attack had no effect on Robonyan.

Jibanyan stepped back and howled as he cradled his injured paws. "Paws of broken bones!"

Nate cringed. "And . . . I think we have a winner."

Whisper nodded. "Looks like Jibanyan 2.0 is superior."

"I won this battle, Jibanyan," Robonyan told him. "But you must still choose to become me in the future, or I will lose the war. Do you understand?"

Jibanyan sighed and slumped away. "Yeah . . ."

With that settled, Nate and the three Yo-kai returned to Nate's house and headed for Nate's room.

"So, uh . . . Robonyan, where are you gonna sleep?" Nate asked nervously.

"My comfort is of no concern, Nate," Robonyan droned. "FOLDING MODE!" With the push of a button, Robonyan turned into a miniature version of himself. "I do not take up much space."

"Aw," Whisper said. "He's even cuter than Jibanyan!"

Robonyan walked over to an outlet. "My batteries can be replenished with a simple household outlet. May I plug in here?"

May I plug in here?

Jibanyan watched as his robo-self plugged in to recharge. He hung his head. "Robonyan really *is* the better version of me."

The next morning, Nate woke to the sound of his mom's voice. "Nate!"

"What is it, Mom?" Nate rubbed his eyes.

"How did you use so much electricity last night?" She sounded furious.

"Huh?" Nate asked. Then he remembered. "Robonyan's batteries!" He spun around just as Robonyan disappeared through a portal in the floor.

"I'll be back," the robot promised.

I'll be back.

Before he disappeared, Robonyan tossed his Yo-kai Medal to Nate.

"Who's gonna pay for all this electricity?" Nate called after him.

But it was too late. Robonyan was gone.

Nate sighed. "I'm glad there's just the real Jibanyan again."

"Who knew Robonyan could consume so much electricity in one night?" Whisper asked.

"Yeah," Nate said. "I guess version 1.0 is better after all." He handed Jibanyan a chocobar.

Jibanyan meowed.

"Here you go. Robonyan may be better at making chocobars, but Jibanyan is better at eating them," Nate said.

"Meow!" Jibanyan said proudly, taking a bite of his chocolate.

"And he's definitely cheaper to have around," Whisper added.

"Wait!" Jibanyan blinked his big cat eyes. "I'm better . . . because I'm *cheaper?*"